Individual contributions are copyright © 2019 Michelle Elvy.
Cover artwork copyright © 2019 Eyayu Genet.

Published by Ad Hoc Fiction.
www.AdHocFiction.com

All rights reserved. No part of this publication may be reproduced, distributed, or transmitted in any form or by any means, including photocopying, recording, or other electronic or mechanical methods, without the prior written permission of the publisher, except in the case of brief quotations embodied in critical reviews and certain other non-commercial uses permitted by copyright law. For permission requests, email the publisher, quoting "Attention Permissions Coordinator" in the subject bar, at the address below:
permissions@adhocfiction.com

Purchasing Information:
Paperback available from www.AdHocFiction.com
E-book available from all usual outlets.

Printed in the United Kingdom.
First Printing 2019.

ISBN paperback 978-1-912095-73-5
ISBN e-book 978-1-912095-51-3

This is a work of fiction. Names, characters, businesses, places, events and incidents are either the products of the author's imagination or used in a fictitious manner. Any resemblance to actual persons, living or dead, or actual events is purely coincidental.

the everrumble

a small novel in small forms

by

Michelle Elvy

for Lola and Jana

Those who still think listening isn't an art should see if they can do it half as well.

—Michael Ende, *Momo*

Advance Praise

A tour de force, Michelle Elvy's the everrumble is a profound, poetic constellation of notes on the Earth's 'alive noises', the hope that lives in the natural world. Zettie's story – her moments of evolving, her capacity to listen and her gift of becoming all the sounds of the earth – affected me to the core.

—CHRISTOPHER ALLEN, author of
Other Household Toxins

Michelle Elvy's acute prose wraps her silent heroine in 'layers of remembered sound', each linked fiction transmitting a luminous sense of the 'loud world' which vibrates her nerve-endings, and tracing her course through a life alert to strange frequencies of experience. the everrumble is a story of listening which makes sound 'touch down' under our scalps, taking our senses on a journey of 'orchestral movement'.

—TRACEY SLAUGHTER, author
of *deleted scenes for lovers*, 2014
Bridport Prize winner

Michelle Elvy's *the everrumble* is an infused and accomplished accumulation of being. The language dances through the reader, elucidating concepts of time and sound and place. In Zettie, acutely conveyed, Elvy gives us a loving homage to our beleaguered planet.

—Catherine McNamara, author of *The Cartography of Others*

With a keen poetic sensibility, *the everrumble* draws the reader into worlds woven with fluidity through time and place. Here is a stunningly original work crackling with an inner and outer expansive life. These linked stories are rife with an elegant gravitas and a unique approach to what is possible once those doors of perception are swung open and one can see, hear and feel what awaits on the other side.

—Robert Scotellaro, author of *What We Know So Far* and *Bad Motel*

What do you hear when you choose to stop speaking? In this glorious and small-but-enormous book, we meet Zettie, born into a cacophonous world with a talent for perceiving sounds too quiet, too far and too deep for the rest of us – including the everrumble. Elvy paints a dreamy, powerful portrait of the life and travels of this word-collector and thinker who becomes celebrated as a visionary, not for seeing but listening. *the everrumble* will leave you filled with questions about what we miss by not paying attention by filling up the silences.

—Tania Hershman, author of
Some Of Us Glow More Than Others

Contents

I

Light and shadow 3
Comfort of a cool pine floor 5
Peek-a-boo 8
Dreamscape I: whale shark and boy 10
Cartwheels 13
The bees 15
The first screaming 18
Fidelity 20
Sea World: August 1971 23
Dreamscape II: moon and sea 24
Before the bees 25
Book Notes 27
Dreamscape III: willow and moon 31
Silence 32
Cartwheels, again 34

Pressure drop, or:
Sea World, August 1971, Part 2 38
The slap 40
Specialists 42
Because 46

II

Soothsayer.......................................51
Higher education 57
Dreamscape IV: bird and warrior 62
Under the Aotearoa sun......................63
Geography......................................66
Birthday...................................... 70
When reading aloud to your children 75
Ways of seeing 78
Dirt...81
Dreamscape V: earth and dust 83
Purity...84
A silence like no other 86
Gifts 88

Dreamscape VI: all of it.................... 90
Kinetic is a frame of mind, really..............91
Dreamscape VII: [untitled] 96
Clarity 97
The everrumble............................101

Acknowledgements 109
About the Author..........................111
About the Artist 113
Story Index 115

I

To hear, one must be silent.

—Ursula LeGuin

Light and shadow

The light enters like tiny diamonds – ancient shards piercing the dark world. Zettie has curled herself so tight she can't feel the fissures anymore; she's smooth like a marble, no sharp edges. Under the woolly cover, she hears her own breath and nothing else. The blanket is blue and green, with streaks of orange
    (papaya, really)
and yellow
    (mango, really)
    and a deep red: primeval soil. It is scratchy on her skin but the whole effect of lying under it creates a smooth muffling. How comforting is the world under cover – those earthy hues touched by sparkling diamond light.

    The blanket's not new. For her birthday today – her seventh – Zettie got a picture book, a plastic doll, a matching plate and cup, all princessy and purple. But the blanket was given to her years ago, back before recollection began – she must have been two, maybe three. For years it sat at the foot of her cot and now today for the first time she fingers it gently, unfolds it and crawls under. She situates herself so her whole body is covered: first she pulls the blanket over her torso, then up over her head, and then, one by one, she pulls in her limbs.

It's no easy task.

As soon as one foot is covered, a hand pokes out. As soon as a hand is tucked in neatly under her chin, a knee pushes sideways and feels the cool of the night air. Finally, after much trying, she manages it, and the very challenge of getting herself completely sheltered, pulling in all her fingers and toes and even the ends of her hair until she can lie there, weightless, becomes the thing that gives her exquisite comfort.

Weightless. Weightless.

This is the year Zettie will live under the blanket. This is the year Zettie stops speaking.

Comfort of a cool pine floor

BOOK NOTES, AGE 8
The Phantom Tollbooth – Norton Juster

> Milo is my new best friend. What is behind him is gone, what is in front of him is nothing. And make-believe is real.

The floor, with its wide pine boards, is smooth and cool. Her fingers run along it and feel the vibrations of the house: the wheezes of the heater in winter, the breezes of the onshore wind in summer.

By the time she is eight, Zettie sleeps on the floor. She feels comfortable there and no bed, no couch, no cot can hold her. Sister Emily has moved to college so she has the room to herself. Her parents rearranged it to make it more hers, to help her settle into the large space. They took out Emily's bookshelves and moved them to the family room;

they removed her single bed and placed it with Brent's just down the hall.

Space, maybe it's space she needs. Maybe quiet. Maybe a room of her own.

But she only needs the wide pine floors. They bring a soft connectedness that cannot be spoken, for beneath them, from beneath the foundation of the house, the earth emits a deep rumble. It will take decades to identify it, this rumble – a noise that would haunt anyone who could hear it. But no one else can. No one but Zettie, ear to pine planking.

On the surface of her days, she hears the movements of her family. Mother is the quietest, gliding up the stairs. Brent takes them two by two and lands with a thud at top or bottom, depending on his direction. Father's steps are predictable – his feet always touch down on the creaking boards in the hallway. You'd think he'd know where the creaks are by now, how to avoid them. But it's a reassuring noise, his *gggrrrk, eerrrrkkk* as he walks up the hallway. For Father is the only one who demands nothing. Brent pokes his sister and tries to get her to giggle, or scream. Mother takes her to speech therapy, wanting to coax words with story time, with sounds of individual vowels or consonants, with experts in smart cashmere sweaters. Zettie likes the consonants, the way they force sound between teeth and tongue, the way the breath, partially obstructed, leaves the mouth.

She spends her time not worrying about whether she'll speak – she knows she won't – but focussed on her study of breath, the way individual particles are expelled from open mouths in front of her. She listens to the Bs, the Ps, the Fs and Ts, the soft play of oxygen, nitrogen and carbon dioxide molecules bumping against each other and speeding along their way to the larger space outside. She likes the Bs and Ps especially, little happy explosions leaving lips. She tries not to smile, for they all look so serious: this is not a smiling matter. But she feels happy, watching the consonants dance forth from the counsellor. The man in the cashmere sweater has no idea how funny he is.

They all try so hard. Except Father – the only one who does not want to prod anything out of her. Father lets her sit in silence, and when he comes down the hallway at night, each night, he comes with a steady, gentle pace, stepping on all the right cracks and creaking in all the right ways, as if to announce himself, and opens her door, and, standing backlit with light shining from around his shoulder and head, says to the child lying on the cool pine floor, 'Goodnight, my silent girl.'

He never asks when her voice will wake.

Peek-a-boo

She wasn't always called Zettie. Her birth name was Marjorie Hanna, after her two grandmothers.

On her second birthday, she was given a blanket by her Aunt Zettie. It was the same colours as Aunt Zettie's hat – wool she'd purchased at the Yarn Barn at a great price, she said. Auntie arrived with the hat on her head and the blanket wrapped in paper with birthday ribbons. When the young girl opened the paper, she pulled the blanket corner up to her eyes and kept it there for a very long time. Then she wrapped it on her head and hid her face. She was at an age when Peek-a-boo made sense: the world was there, and she was here. Even if she didn't know what *here* was – it was the place where her molecules were assembled under one cover, with none of them flowing outward or escaping to float away in the spirally air currents she could sense all around her dark head. The adults in the room clapped their hands, laughing every time she peeked out and surprised them. They could not guess at her joy in the long moments under the blanket.

There, here – the separation was supreme.

When she peeked out the first time, moon eyes shining, her brother Brent, who was five at the time, pointed back and forth between Auntie and his sister and said, *Big Zettie, Little Zettie.*

Little Zettie wore the blanket on her head all day and the name stuck.

She sometimes dreamed of colours floating, and the way the blanket smelled: sky, sea, earth. She slept with it at the foot of her bed. It grounded her to earth and even then, even at such a young age, before vocabulary forms and expresses the meaning of connections and groundings, it was as if she needed something to keep her there. As if the blanket held her in one place – if she let it go, she may float up to the sky and never come back down. She crawled under the blanket at night and felt the weight of it, holding her there. Anchoring her to earth.

And soon, she stopped peeking out.

The world was there, and she was here.

Dreamscape I:
whale shark and boy

She dreamed she was a whale shark dreaming he was a boy dreaming he was a whale shark dreaming he was a boy dreaming he was a whale shark dreaming he was a boy. Illuminating. Diving. Soaring. All in one night, or maybe it was one hour, or even one minute. She dove down down down and found fluorescent charms swinging from the snouts of seahorses. She flew firecrackerfast, fearsome and jubilant at the dizzying depths and the iridescent shape of things. She fed on plankton but they weren't plankton at all – they were morsels of delight, merry magical minstrels skipping on her tongue, pressing and lifting at the same time. Between bites (gapes, because there's no chewing when you're a whale shark) she napped and dreamed, and she was the boy, and she had a ladder, and she climbed and climbed and climbed. The ladder went up to the top of her house and beyond. It touched treetops and the salt of the sea-sky in the harbour. It exceeded the reach of her mother's call, way out in the everdark of the night. She dove through silk raindrops and she was a whale shark again, pectoral fin browsing slippery sand. And then she was a boy again. Shifting back and forth, down and up: first tail swish, long and smooth and elegant like a shark but not a shark, then boy with hands – hands! – digging a mote of water for protection (naturally) around a castle, singing sea-lavender songs. As a whale shark, she dreamed the boy, and as a boy, she dreamed the whale shark. And so on. Blueblack of ocean to

blackblue of sky. Down and back up. Swimming laddering lunging climbing.

She can be anything in her dreams.

She opens her mouth and swallows the stars.

Cartwheels

BOOK NOTES, AGE 6
Pippi Longstocking – Astrid Lindgren

I love Pippi. Pippi can do anything.

The girls are spinning. Round and round they go, fingers clasped and ponytails flying. They clutch each other's small hands so tight their fingers turn red, but they dare not let go. The world flies by at astonishing speed, a blur of yellows and greens and blues and the dull grey of neighbourhood houses.

When Scott comes into view – suddenly it's yellow-green-blue-grey-scott-yellow-green-blue-grey-scott – Zettie lets go and Sally is sent back on her heels and bottom, then onto her elbows where she slams to a halt.

Scott is Zettie's brother's best friend. He walks by coolly, smiles at Zettie, says, *Can you do a cartwheel?*

She tries, lands on her bottom next to Sally.

Without saying anything, Scott puts down his backpack and hurls himself over once, twice, three times, four. He goes round and round the girls, feet over hands over feet over hands over feet over hands. When he's gone all the way around, he picks up his backpack again and goes into the house. Cool like that.

Sally scrambles to her feet, mutters, *Show off.*

Zettie stands up and smoothes her striped t-shirt over her pink terrycloth shorts, tries it again.

The bees

A buzzing. Not the everyday buzzings – those are there too but this is more.

    She hears beyond those usual house hums, beyond the lawnmower and sprinkler, beyond the boy sneezing while he paints the fence next door and beyond the car that won't start down the street. She hears beyond the baby crying at the community pool and the girls jumping rope at the end of the shady lane. She hears those too. It's a hot summer day and some houses are closed up with air conditioning, their units spitting in their drip-drip way, and she hears those as well, but her house doesn't have air con so the windows are open to the stifling heat that claws through every room. She hears the grumble of a large vehicle and knows it's the garbage truck, eight streets away, or is it ten, in the newly developed part of the neighbourhood, the one with cul de sacs and neatly sculpted sidewalk plantings.

    It's beyond them, this buzzing, beyond the park on the other side of town, beyond town itself. It's beyond beyond beyond.

She lifts her head from the pine floorboard in her upstairs bedroom and cocks it to one side, her left ear tuned to whatever is sliding along the heated airwaves herward. Drifting in through the window on that slightest of breeze comes this higher-pitched hum, something so small she almost misses it. But it announces itself to her; it has a reason for arriving. She's too young to know that yet – she's only five – but she senses that sounds seek her out, and she knows she ought to do her best to listen. Even if it's just a faraway buzzing.

She listens a full five minutes before she realises it's the bees in Aunt Zettie's yard, out in the county. Aunt Zettie has kept bees for years, since way before Little Zettie was born. Her honey is legendary. People come from all around to buy it at the farmers' market each month. Little Zettie never misses a chance to visit the hive and watch the merry industry of the creatures. One summer she tried to name them all, using names that only began with B: Bernard, Billy, Bruce, Ben, Brad, Beau, Brendan, Brady, Blake, Bob, Byron. There was one who stung her three times and she named him after her brother Brent.

Zettie loves going to see the bees. But she goes only once a month because Aunt Zettie lives too far away – farther than a walk, farther than a bus ride.

Under the bee buzz is something else. A low rumble. It bores gently into her ear and winds down the canal, vibrating through her whole body, her throat, her chest, her tummy. It moves out to the tips of her limbs, to the very ends of her long brown hair. Once she hears it she can't un-hear it.

The rumble is here to stay.

The first screaming

She was an October baby, and 1965 was a noisy place, except for the Ed White's space walk which was of course silent in the purest sense of the word. But the world Zettie was born into was – there's no other word for it – loud. The Who belted out their first album; The Beatles released *Help!*. The US unleashed a bombing campaign in Vietnam and later sent ground troops. Malcolm X was shot; Martin Luther King Jr marched. Tear gas was unleashed in Selma; Watts was ravaged. Thousands paid tribute to Sir Winston Churchill, thousands cheered for West Ham. Julie Andrews sang her heart out from a set that looked like the Austrian Alps and Cher hit big time with her first TV appearance. The word *fuck* shook the media world. Rhodesia declared independence. An earthquake rocked Seattle, an underground explosion killed 31 in Wales. Cyclones ravaged India and Hurricane Betsy struck Florida and Louisiana. It was the age of nuclear testing, and America hummed with 76 million cars on its highways. Peter Jennings reported it all on The Nightly News.

But above all that – those history-making events that get recorded and noted and examined and discussed – there was something else on Zettie's birthday. A screaming that happened concurrent with her birth – something no other person in the world heard but that drifted in through the open hospital window and vibrated her timpanic membrane.

She had no way of identifying it, of course, because how can you identify anything over the suckingslurpingslipping surroundsound of your own birth? But when she opened her mouth and wailed she wondered, in her newborn-no-words-but-conscious-oh-yes-I'm-conscious way, if it was her own scream or someone else's she was exhaling with such force.

It would take some time before she'd come back to that scream.

It would take some time to get used to the world she was born into.

Such cacophony.

Fidelity

BOOK NOTES, AGE 12
The Adventures of Huckleberry Finn – Mark Twain

> Give me a raft, set me adrift. Sometimes I lie back on the kayak on the lake, and look up at the sky and imagine what Huck can see from his raft. It must be the same sky, the same stars.

Emily is home from college, a kaleidoscope of colour in her new clothes, new hair, new nails. She has a new boyfriend, too – makes her face rosyfresh. Zettie is only twelve and uninterested. But she likes seeing her sister happy so she decides to be her best self. She smiles at her sister's stories. She shows her sister her marked-up copy of *Franny and Zooey*, which Emily gave her at Christmas, and notes the important passages. *She was not one for emptying her face of expression.* That one made them both fall on the bed together, delighted and holding their stomachs with giggles. Snorty ones from Emily, shoulder-shaky from Zettie.

A mosquito flies through a broken screen three streets down. Zettie hears the wingbeat, 111 times per second.

And when she hears the motorbike pull into the drive and sees her sister's face so round with expectation, she too feels a little jolt in her chest.

The mosquito selects the arm of a sleeping baby boy, succulent and new. Zettie has read that mosquitoes like the carbon dioxide we exhale, the way it combines with fatty acids and uric acid and lactic acid. Baby's breath must signal a feast, she thinks.

She focusses on the mosquito several houses down the street. It helps block the closer noises. She tries not to listen to her sister and the boyfriend but can't help herself. Their voices are muffled but everything else is deafening: the quick, wet smacking of lips parting and teeth tugging. Those things prick her skin.

She watches from the upstairs bathroom window when Emily and her boyfriend say their goodbyes to each other in the dark hours of the night. When

Emily turns to go inside, the boyfriend reaches out for Emily's ponytail, pulls it gently. She's in his arms again. Zettie feels a pang of jealousy, just a little.

She keeps to herself when she hears the *vrrooommm* of his motorbike peel away and grow faint and then accelerate and travel out into the countryside. She hears it shift down as it climbs hills and break before curves, how it accelerates on straightaways. She can hear the wind whistling, tickling his neck, blowing the curls that whip from the sides of the helmet. She hears him as he travels all the way to the next town, where the motorcycle finally comes to a halt and, kickstand barely down, is greeted by another girlish voice, slightly higher-pitched than her sister's. And then: more soft sucking sounds, a low grunt she does not know.

And: another mosquito, thirsty in the sticky night air, scenting new blood, somewhere nearby.

Sea World: August 1971

Kids shouting mothers swearing fathers sweating strollers strolling snack carts squeaking hawkers hawking guitar humming bass thrumming feet stomping drums drumming.

Ice cream dripping orange peel brrriiipppping turtles racing lemonade sourfacemaking wind whistling steaks sizzling corn popping newborn napping feet flapping palms clapping.

Heat frazzling cola sprizzling apples crunching Twizzlers twizzling.

Leavers leaving stayers staying night coming sun end-of-daying.

And a long insistent howl that pitches high above the rest of the day's noise and travels out across the San Diego hills. Shamu was captured in 1965, October. A young female orca taken from the wild. Now, a cry echoes across the busy harbour, into the crystal blue world that Shamu dreams as she dies.

Dreamscape II:
moon and sea

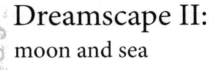

She is the moon and the sea. She holds a jar – a gift from her sister. In it all the earth's water, and in the water all the earth's sorrow. Which floats and lifts on the gentle swells – sometimes it's smaller and fragments are caught in the breeze, lifted and blown away. Sometimes it's heavy enough, solid, to puncture the sea's surface, to break through the thin veneer that separates liquid from sky, and sink through the deep, down down down, to the ocean floor. But sorrow can't be drowned, no. It must be lifted and floated again. So she pulls on the sea with her moon eyes and moon breast, and sorrow rises, rises again, to the surface, where she can watch it all night long.

Before the bees

BOOK NOTES, AGE 4
The Very Hungry Caterpillar – Eric Carle

HUN8Ry cATRpILA r

Before the bees there were other noises. Some things she was not meant to hear. Things like people shouting at each other. Mothers scolding their children. BB guns and sling shots. And once she heard Uncle Roger's low moan that was animal-like and urgent and when she cocked her head to the side and listened closer she realised it was not Aunt Zettie's voice, but a whiny high-pitched one that accompanied Roger's low braying. She covered her ears and tried to un-listen but the sound kept coming, *uh uh uuuuuh uuuuuh.* She focussed further out. She found a fly on a windowsill two houses down, opened her ears to him.

She settled her mind's eye on the small fly as it tried to find the exit and buzzed frantically in the corner of the pane. Bzzzz bzzzz bzzzz.

The fly buzzed out the window, finally, only to land near a manmade pond behind the Selwyns' house where later that afternoon he was snapped up by a snapping turtle. Zettie heard that too. She was getting used to hearing all these small sounds – and she was listening more and more for them, even for the terrible clap of the turtle's jaws. And, at dusk, the near-quiet movements of the lurking raccoon, keen for a moment to lunge at the turtle's moist eggs. For these were live sounds, natural sounds. Far more appealing than the sounds Uncle Roger made.

Book Notes

The book was a gift – her fourth birthday. A small book with butterflies on the front cover. From her dad. He also gave her crayons. There were no lines in the book so she was free to draw in it as she pleased. She drew a small caterpillar and copied the words from the first page of her favourite book: *The Very Hungry Caterpillar*. The letters were thick, in black crayon, sometimes upper case, sometimes lower case. It brought her tremendous satisfaction, this compiling of lines and circles to form letters to form words to form meaning. As much joy as the little green worm himself, replicated there on her notebook page.

Two years later, her mother gave her a book that was to become treasured, too: *Pippi Longstocking*. She loved the girl who could defy gravity, with her muscle-man strength and her sticky-outy pigtails. She drew countless images of this gangly heroine in her new book. And she took her sister's pencil set and wrote notes in meticulous penmanship (for a six-year-old): *Things Pippi can do: definitely*. And she listed all of Pippi's adventures, one by one, and even the ones she had not yet tried but aimed to.

Which was the end of Zettie's drawing career and the beginning of her true love of words. Words that had far more meaning than the state of the caterpillar's stomach on any given day. His little story was neat, charming in its own way, but this? Pippi opened up a world of ideas to her. A world of possibles. When she wrote Pippi's remarkable doings in coloured pencils, thinner and more precise than the black crayon squiggles, they came alive on the page, the word *definitely* shaped so determinedly and offering such grand potential.

Zettie spent hours in her room, reading books and collecting words. At night she kept her light on as long as she was allowed, then buried herself under her covers. *You can' t stay up after dark*, they said. But the dark had no hold on her – she felt light burn inside, deep in her solar plexus, when she scribbled in her notebook. An aliveness that lit up the world.

And a year later, when she stopped talking, not only did the world become louder in all ways but it also brightened, all senses turned up a notch. Everything was alight day and night – and grownups, as far as she could tell, seemed not to notice.

She soon learned that Pippi's adventures, and all that possibility, had been written first in a language that looked entirely different than her own.

And the girl who uttered that phrase also had a different name: Pippi Långstrump.

Such a new idea, that someone might be called something else in a somewhere else.

This she pondered for many years, pulling books from library shelves and looking for extraordinary names, in her own tongue and in others. Characters from books became her companions: Babar and Momo (such names were full and round in her mouth) and Mrs Pepperpot and Amelia Bedelia and Eeyore and Fiver and Bilbo and Milo. She noted them all in her notebooks in her characteristically careful print.

And the idea of *there, here*: how it haunted her, drove her forward. What was over there? How did it look, compare to here? Worlds larger than her own. Worlds hidden. Worlds in pages of books, worlds in the beyond. Places she could find if she only learned how to look for them, how to hear them.

Thereafter she began collecting book notes as she read, adding to her first entry and crowding her little book with letters that fascinated her. As her knowledge of languages grew, she kept one book that had special notations – the ones she pulled out repeatedly. There was Little Tiger, catching two fish so that he might eat one and put the other back – a gift of life, and such joy (*Janosch, Post für den Tiger*); and arguments about truth and perception (Flaubert/ Nadeau). Also proverbs such as *giza likizidi, kucha kunakaribia – when darkness becomes more intense, dawn is near*: useful in many applications.

In the margins of the pages, she also developed the habit of adding phrases she turned in her mind, over and over; phrases like *Man lernt nie aus* (German, *you never stop learning*); *Fingertoppskänsla* (Swedish, *finger tips moving*, or *intuitively thinking*) and *Hapana bahari isiyo mawimbi* (Kiswahili, *there is no sea without waves*).

And this, her favourite word: *levande ljus* (Swedish), for candle. *Living light*.

Dreamscape III:
willow and moon

She leans over to touch her toes – a yogic stretch – and the wind whistles through her branches for now she is a tree, bending like a willow. She folds herself to catch the sorrow in her branches (see it? it's down there, hovering in the earthen dirt, brown and red and gold and black and all the world's colours) but as she moves to scoop it up with her branches, sinewy and soft, it floats upward on a kick of breeze, an updraft, and now she opens her moon heart and pulls it back in, envelops it in an embrace that gives it light, and now she's willow and moon, holding sorrow in her supple arms and sending light up to the heavens and down through her roots and all roots of all trees.

Silence

BOOK NOTES, AGE 15
The Dream of a Common Language – Adrienne Rich

> Silence as a blueprint to a life... I've been reading Adrienne Rich. My English teacher assigns novels and plays, but the images in poetry hold water. Slippery, and beautiful. Silence is a whole world – a voice, too.

> And silence is not absence.

Uncle Roger knew she wouldn't talk. Her silence drew him to her – and also almost made him stop. Her silence, heartbreaking under the weight of his hips, but not loud enough to lift him from the bed. His knees ground into the plaid flannel bedsheets, and he looked away. They were thin, the sheets, smelling of lavender and sweat, and something like sweet corn or carrots lingered on her breath

– the soup she had eaten for dinner, perhaps. As he pumped and pumped the smell of that gently chewed corn and carrots assaulted his nostrils, took him to the messy meals on the plastic tray in front of his daughter, only one year old: the way she smeared everything in her hair and laughed when they tried to clean her off. He pushed her from his mind and slid his spider fingers over the snowy body beneath him.

That girl's silence followed him to work, followed him to his Thursday night poker game. It came along fly fishing on Saturday, working its way to his fingers where it froze them mid-tie, leaving the Woolly Bugger knotted and unfinished. It was with him, too, when a fly-ball came ripping into the stands at a Philadelphia Phillies game – near the end of the season, the same season they won game six against the Kansas City Royals and took the World Series. He reached for the ball and thought for a brief moment he had it. And then it slipped through his spider fingers.

When he died only three years later, she hurled her silence to him one last time, screaming down his ear.

Cartwheels, again

BOOK NOTES, AGE 14
'Hope is the thing with feathers' — Emily Dickinson

It's all in the title.

She'd mastered the cartwheel at age six. She practiced all day one afternoon and into the evening, till her pink terrycloth shorts were smeared with grass stains and her small arms ached. These days, she can circle the front lawn with her eyes closed while her best friend Sally Hula-hoops to Fleetwood Mac. When her brother and his friend Scott turn up, Sally swings her hips harder and puts on a fine show.

Zettie cartwheels away.

Now the girls are sitting on the greying wooden porch steps and a general malaise has landed over them like a mid-summer sigh. The breeze is too thin, and Zettie can see the sweat sliding down Sally's temple. Sally's talking about Ted in school. Ted who has a new skateboard, Ted who has new Star Wars cards, Ted who has grown taller this summer, did you notice?

Zettie is silent.

Sally, who needs no retort from her friend, goes inside through the screen door and brings back two glasses of tea.

I like your mom's tea better than my mom's, Sally says, putting the glass to her cheek and tinkling the ice cubes. *All that sugar, and mint. And your mom uses real lemons. Mine uses lemon juice from a glass bottle that we keep in the fridge door.*

Zettie smiles, signs a quick reference that she knows her friend will get, then puckers her lips in an exaggerated way. Sally giggles, says, *Of course I remember!*

They're laughing about the time they were little, when they were playing one of their favourite games, the one where you have to close your eyes and guess what you're drinking. Zettie had swallowed a whole spoonful of lemon juice concentrate; her face contorted in a sour pucker and then she fell off her stool. Sally knew that was the sign that she'd won – and she fell down next to her friend and they lay on the kitchen floor, together, holding their stomachs and laughing till tears spilled down their faces.

The look on your face, Sally says now. *I'll never forget it!*

Zettie takes the glasses inside, washes them in the kitchen sink. She's about to dry them when Brent comes through the screen door and says, *Leave them, we'll use them.* Behind him is Scott. Zettie has known Scott for as long as she can remember – for as long as she's known Sally, probably. His house is two streets over but he practically lives at their house during summer. She likes having two older brothers. Especially because Scott is nicer than Brent. And smells grassy and green. And has grown taller this summer, did you notice?

Zettie stands just inside the doorway when the boys go out with their baseball gloves and ball. She can hear Scott breathing softly and the brown leathery smell of his glove floats on the light evening breeze. She likes the thud of the ball hitting the gloves, a rhythmic to and fro, a repeated leaving and arriving connected by an arc that spans the space between the two friends – sometimes high and elongated, sometimes a flatter more direct means of arriving, but always geometrically balanced.

She sneezes and unintentionally breaks the rhythm.

It's then that Scott drops his glove to the ground and stretches his suntanned arms high overhead before launching himself sideways and forward, feet over hands over feet over hands over feet over hands, in a fast-flowing and seamless circle, all the way around the front lawn, then arriving back at the place where he started, where he retrieves his glove, slides it onto his left hand in the same way he's done a thousand and more times and winks at the girl behind the screen door.

Then he hollers, *Play ball!* and throws the ball in another perfect arc.

Pressure drop, or: Sea World, August 1971, Part 2

A screaming, of a different kind. Not a jet or a rocket or anything else high-pitched and man-made. This was something organic, a pressing need, an urgency that compressed molecules and made barometers fall.

Zettie was six when she first understood the cry of another animal. It came from across the continent. She heard the accompanying, and more obvious, noises of the day – mothers, fathers, toddlers, strollers, ice creams, sunset – but this sound rose above everything else and reached around the circumference of the globe. It started in San Diego and went out into the great Pacific Ocean, sailing on the tradewinds west, across the wide blue expanse. It sailed as far as it could, now moving and eddying, now lingering in the doldrums. Part of it blew into the northern Pacific and fragmented further, soaring back to North America and then urgently over the mountainous inland terrain, all the way to the Atlantic. Ocean to ocean, continent over continent. Unrelenting and urgent. It went north and south, too. A piece of it is still lodged in Antarctic ice. Particles hover at both poles.

It was while passing across the northeast of North America, across Lake Munson, Maine, that it reached the small girl named Zettie, and found its way into her ear, drilling deep and vibrating her teeth. She was drinking a glass of milk when it arrived on a soft summer drift and touched down under her scalp.

Shamu was dead after only six years in captivity. And now her cry would dwell in that layer of remembered sound, something real and everlasting to those who listen.

The glass of milk slipped from the small girl's fingers. The sky crushed in on itself and let forth a shatter of rain.

The slap

BOOK NOTES, AGE 9
Where the Sidewalk Ends – Shel Silverstein

> Brent likes the one about the boy who loses his head. Emily keeps saying in a funny voice: Sarah Cynthia Sylvia Stout Would Not Take The Garbage Out.

> Must ask for new chalk this summer. I will draw arrows on our sidewalk and walk off the edge.

The slap echoes across the park, so loud she can't understand why no one else has heard it. The other noises mask it, she supposes. The other noises are jubilant and summery: the crack of a bat, the swoop of barn swallows, the glug of a 7-11 Slurpee, grape, sliding down Jenny Carroll's skinny neck. Feet running around dusty bases, cheers going up in the scattered crowd. Her brother and Jim Whitman toking behind Mrs Henderson's Buick station wagon.

When she hears it, she jerks her head up and starts her eyes skimming. When she finally settles on the place the noise has come from, she sees a young couple she does not know, a man and a woman standing close to each other, facing one another, the afternoon September sun backlighting them, speckled shadows dancing on their shoulders. They are there, beyond the ballpark, beyond the chain link fence, under a maple tree, its colours already turning, at the edge of the parking-lot pavement.

The woman holds her palm to her cheek, looks up at the man, who places his hand over hers.

From where Zettie stands, they look perfect.

Specialists

BOOK NOTES, AGE 13
Charlotte's Web – E.B. White

> If you don't pay attention you might miss all the animals talking. They are talking morning, noon and night. They're always talking. So loud.
>
> But then again, so are people.

She is tired of specialists. Specialists who want her to speak, specialists who want to know why she stopped in the first place. Specialists who discuss the plasticity of the brain, who scan and label and scan some more. Possible causes for speech stoppage (an entirely new term developed for her special case; causes listed in lab technicians' notebooks over the years): low frequency disturbance, a rattling of the eardrum causing psychological inhibitors to speech. Ventilation calibrations. Suburban vibrations.

Magnetic resonances, atmospheric interferences. Limbic imbalance, cataclysmic stress.

That's it. They think she's cataclysmically stressed.

They like to ask her to 'rate' noise on a scale, from 'Not annoying' to 'Extremely annoying'.

She smiles. *You are all extremely annoying.*

Life is infinitely more interesting than examining what is perceived as her problem. In school there are field trips to the tidal pools and French irregular verbs. Diagramming sentences and Euclidean relations. All of those are far more interesting than the people who want to make Zettie speak. It has been six full years since she put a stop to her tongue, and she does not miss it. Since then she has tuned into the earth, and she's learning this year to concentrate on sounds she characterises as *alive*. Dead noises are things like airplanes, construction sites, fire whistles and police sirens. They make her tired, numb.

Infrasound, on the other hand: now that's interesting. Weather across a distant ocean, surf on a beach a thousand miles away, an avalanche in the Rockies, an iceberg calving in Alaska. Seismic growling others can't hear. In the last year alone she has heard the earth shift over a thousand times. Not that she's counting. It's more a sense of scale. Who counts when the number's that high – besides the scientists in their perfectly ironed labcoats. She wrote a school report about the Miyagi earthquake that occurred in June. She had all the book-facts right, all the things she could collect from newspaper reports she found in the school library. She got an A – teacher held her work up as an example for the class. But her description of the plates shifting was not satisfactory, to her: how to capture the sound of more than 1000 houses she heard crack open and crumble and squash and slip and fall? The terrific noise of landslides. The charts and scales and diagrams she painted in black and blue and red were less than mere approximations of the sounds of the earth breaking open.

Since that report, she's been choosing to focus on sounds that feel more alive. She keeps a notebook.

Alive noises, today: frogs chirping, whales humming, crickets preening, pigs snorting, mosquitoes mating, elk singing, bears gawomping. Batsong and birdsong. Woodpeckers on a tin roof: snare drum. Also: bushes whispering, trees weeping, rain thundering, lightning zinging, stones clattering, thunder roaring, waterfalls shattering, clouds sighing.

There is a screaming, besides all that. She notes it in her notebook every time she thinks of it, but she's yet to resolve its mystery. It is Shamu, she's almost sure, a high-pitched reverberation. But how can that be? She heard Shamu die that day in August 1971. She heard it from her bedroom in quiet Lake Munson, Maine. It was one of those early childhood moments, from a time back before she decided to stop speaking. Something like that will change a six-year-old. There she was, combing her pretty doll's plastic hair, when that shriek landed through her window. She tuned in and heard everything that was happening that day at Sea World: the kids, the ice cream, the sweaty fathers and hurrying mothers, the splashing and flopping. And then: that impossible cry, Shamu dead.

And now this: not a death call, but equally desperate. It comes from a place muffled and dark. She makes a note under Other Animal Noises. She'll come back to it. It's a mystery that will unfold itself in time.

That and the *everrumble* she dreams each night.

Because

Let's talk about the word because. It follows the word why and waits, expectantly, for the rest.

For years, Zettie's mother tried to find the answer to the question why. She looked in books, in cereal boxes, in sugar, in milk. She asked the question to anyone who would listen: professionals, neighbours, her own mother. She asked God. She asked the Devil. She asked the tallest tree in the garden. She shrieked her why, she cried her why.

And still the girl wouldn't speak.

As for the girl herself, she had no answer, nor did she seek it. She heard the question Why every day for years. But unlike her mother, she knew the silence that followed Because was enough. There was nothing after that. The air after Because became a cushiony comfort: a knowing in the not-knowing. A soft billowing thing that filled the space with expectation and – not dread, no – hope.

Why do we have to know the why? The because is infinite.

THE EVERRUMBLE

II

Life begins before a soul is born and
commences once again with the act of dying.

—Peter Mattiessen

Soothsayer

BOOK NOTES, AGE 99
Momo – Michael Ende

> I must have been a very young girl when I first encountered the magic of Michael Ende. I read The Neverending Story, yes. But it's Momo I read over and over – the young girl whose story I wrote into English and who speaks to me, always. Who is timeless herself. There's a moment that I keep coming back to: when Momo hears time. But it's not the noise of everyone's time, of Time with a capital T – it's her own time. It's Professor Hora (who else?) who reveals it to her. He shows her how to measure it, how to hear it. To understand it. Her eyes and ears can't see or hear it. For it's something she carries with her always: deep in her heart, her soul. In her very being.
>
> Time and truth – elusive but central to our existence. Poets and storytellers, philosophers

and historians: we all seek it. My life is not so much about truth but honesty – and I think there is a difference, for truth can be thought about as an absolute, while honesty is simply a way of being. My own life goal is closer to something I read by Maya Angelou, something that stays with me: to be honest, and to hope that honesty has guided me through my life, to think clearly about my path. It's the central notion of honesty that has given me courage to see, to touch, to feel, to smell the very world I live in. And to hear.

In time the girl called Little Zettie would come to be known as a soothsayer, a visionary. Not because she could see the future but because she knew how to listen to all the sounds of the earth. In Belitung one year, in the Java Sea, between Bali and Singapore, she was led to the Dukun so he could see into her eyes for himself. He asked her to hold out her hands, and when he took them she felt the waterfall tumbling nine kilometers away. She was offered a bed at the Dukun's house but she found her way to the waterfall instead and slept there for three weeks, ear to the ground and open to the smallest trickles under the tickling wet moss. On the island of Java some time after that, she would join the pilgrimage to Genung Kemukus for prayer and, while others engaged in sexual rituals that accompanied the gathering, she was left entirely alone under the stars, her silence piercing the noise of the crazed sweaty throng.

And in New Zealand, where she settled for a number of years, they referred to her as the girl with an ancient story, *he kōrero tūārangi*, not because she told any story at all but because there was an energy emanating from her, hollowed out in the space immediately around her and trailing behind her.

When she finally settled in one place more than a few years, long after her time in New Zealand and Central America and northern Europe, she came to be regarded with an easy distance by the residents of this small East African village, who eventually turned to her with offerings, looking for signs. They brought her roosters, eggs, cloth, walking sticks. They carved knotty wood into beautiful shapes for her. They pressed mint into water, squeezed juice made from tamarind. The children brought driftwood and shells they collected on the shore, made stools and small digging tools for her garden. They repaired her small mud hut when the sun baked it dry and cracked it open at the seams, hauling buckets of water from the well to pack in new wet soil that would hold another season. When they made the first repair, she placed one of the children's shells into the soft mud and there it stayed, glinting in the sun. Thereafter, every time the children brought shells, they'd choose the shiniest ones and press them into the sides of the hut.

She would, in turn, listen to their stories, stories that extended past the hour when the dark pulled up its stars. They called her *Ng'aa*, the woman who shines. This was a term of endearment and used somewhat ironically, of course, because she was not new and fancy and pretty but one who seemed as old as the earth itself. The villagers had a sense of humour about her – they had to, for the alternative was to fear her mightily.

Because when she squatted on her front stoop, with those small shells forming circles round the house, they could see a shine all around her. It was as if they forgot they had put the shells there in the first place; once there, they became part of the house, part of her. And when she put her ear to the ground and listened, they knew she was hearing the earth speak to her from deep in its crevices, down where fire and wind and water and air dwell at their source. Down where their ancestors dwell. Down where all the world began.

Sometimes they would see her thin exterior ripple in the light, its myriad wrinkles moving, and they sensed that the story of the world lived under her skin.

Sometimes, when she put her ear to the ground, she could tell them, with a nod of her head, or a sad shake, whether mtoto would live or die – not because she could see into the future (because she was not a seer) but because she could hear the minutest of all living things, even the flutter of a heart so small and worn already with the weight of trying that it would give out. She could hear mtoto's last try, the wee heart's last beat.

Just yesterday such a child was brought to her. And though she was sad for the small girl and her keening parents, she did as she always did, as the people of the village had come to expect, for she had lived among them for decades by then: she held the tiny figure and let the parents cry in front of her, and she listened to what she knew would be the baby's last breaths, before she handed the bundle back to the parents with shoulders that would now always be a little more bent, and knelt to the earth and placed her hands on the hard packed soil, then bent over from the waist and put her ear to the ground and stayed there for a long minute. There she heard the earth speak to her – the distant rumble, the *everrumble* – and she raised her head up and offered what might be interpreted as a smile.

And the parents of the small girl who had stopped breathing by then did not exactly smile but felt reassured that this powerful woman, this shiny woman who devoted her life to listening to the earth, had listened to them, too.

Higher education

BOOK NOTES, AGE 38
Letters to a Young Poet – Rainer Maria Rilke
   and
'Sleeping with a Dictionary' – Harryette Mullen

> I think it's important to ask the questions, but not to ask for the answers.
>
> Perhaps it's about serendipity: if you live life with your own enduring questions, you will, sooner or later, happen upon answers. All possible paths lead from one place – and that is the heart within.
>
> I'm reading these poets together. Books in my bed, on the pillow beside me – a habit since I was a young girl. Sounds sink in during sleep. Words meander, migrate, move. Rilke morphs with Mullen. Language pushes past the darkening light and moves, weightless, in my dreams.

Language became the thing Zettie loved more than anything else. Which sounds funny for a person who doesn't speak, but the sounds she heard, the roll and thunder and quiet shuffle on the page – those reverberated like a second heartbeat. Language was both predictable and surprising. The structures of it, the frameworks, the very positioning of the verb in a sentence. In university, she studied Swedish and French and German and graduated with high honours. She didn't *speak* languages but she *understood* them. She translated academic articles for professors, who saw her facility as a gift from God – even her atheist German professor. She learned to tune out the rest of the world and listen to what was there on the page in front of her, almost as if she could hear each individual author. And it was not a lonely business, because she could now surround herself with voices she chose, voices that brought pleasure and cracked open questions, even questions unanswerable. A treatise on love, a powerful argument against communism by an economist who was anything but a capitalist, a call for universal rights of trees (outlandish and wonderful). She giggled her way through a French author writing a response to Mark Twain's essay on 'The Awful German Language' and made friends, mentally, with a woman who tried to diagram every sentence in her head, as she heard it, as a focussing exercise – who found herself in everyday conversation mapping direct and indirect objects and prepositional phrases and dependent clauses with all their descending segments. Zettie tried it too, went about mapping the people around her, and she came, for a time, to think of each individual person as a noun or a verb or an adverb or – the unlucky ones – an indefinite article. Woe to the person reduced to a mere *a*!

The first book she translated into English was one she was especially proud of: Astrid Lindgrin's *Titta, Madicken, det snöar! – The Runaway Sleigh Ride*. Thereafter she translated several children's books but eventually shifted to adult works, mostly Swedish and German, but occasionally she was asked to do a comparative analysis between German and French for an academic studying Swiss folk tales. That lasted many years – he kept coming back – and she often felt like she could hear the exquisitely elliptical phrasings moving back and forth between French and German from Bern all the way to her. She would spend what became a career translating new editions of Hesse, Rilke and Mann, and she would come to translate the 100th anniversary edition of *The Magic Mountain*, a feat larger than any other of her projects. For a while her focus was Nelly Sachs, and the idea of *Fahrt ins Staublose* – Journey into the dustless realm – led to deeper excavations of her own sense of self. But the project that brought the most joy to her heart was translating a book from German to English about a girl who saves her village from Men in Grey who come to steal Time. She translated Michael Ende's *Momo* for the occasion of its 30th anniversary of publication, to accolades and awards.

She lived a quiet life, sometimes in cities as bustling as Singapore or Stockholm, sometimes in remote islands in the Indian Ocean. She moved around the world with her two daughters. She had a loving distance relationship with their father. She was content and had learned to tune into the things that mattered, and to leave the rest alone. She enjoyed the sounds that filled her mind and body, the ardent philosophies of companions from book manuscripts: Settembrini and Naphta, Beppo and Guido. And Pippi – always Pippi.

But something else happened during the *Momo* translation. Something that pulled her into a trance in the early hours of each day, listening to time itself. When she was translating Ende's pages, each sentence, each word and fragment, slipping under her skin in her sleep, she felt the low rumbling she'd always felt, ancient and insistent, resonating in her bones. She resorted to sleeping on the floor of her cottage, listening to a rumble that came in waves – a rumble that transcended the physicality of space and the linear construct of time.

And one night she expanded her ribs, just enough to make them stretch and creak a little, and moved her mind into the dark place of something in her core, and rumbled back.

This was something beyond words. Way beyond.

Dreamscape IV:
bird and warrior

She is bird and she is warrior she is bird and she is warrior she is both and they are they are they are and then they aren't and then they are again, over and over and over and and and and and and

Under the Aotearoa sun

BOOK NOTES, AGE 24
The Bone People – Keri Hulme

> Oh, how I love the idea that hands are sacred. That touch is a thing of love – fingertips feeling for eyes that cannot see, for mouths that do not speak.

They said she'd break Rangi's heart; they knew as soon as she arrived that her life was in motion, that she wasn't meant to stay.

But the two were like sea and sky together. And who could argue against sea and sky?

She was only twenty-four when she arrived in New Zealand and after she left they began to recall her with great vividness, and they did so for years. Not only because she bore Rangi's children (wild like fresh gorse in the heaving hills of Whangarei Heads), and not only because those two children in turn gave them seven grandchildren and, eventually, twelve great-grandkids, and more after that. But also because she was the girl whose silence could knock you over, the girl who bore the moon and the sea in her eyes and the trees in her limbs and the bees and birds and all flying creatures in her heart.

The girl who talked with her hands.

They remembered her hands, and her skin. There was something about how her skin moved and changed. For her face never revealed much, but her skin turned fiercely dark under the powerful Aotearoa sun, and it was noted by all that she seemed to be, in appearance, not European and not Polynesian and not anything else familiar, but something dark and shadowy, something earthly and solid and rooted to the world down to its very heart. The way her skin moved on her bones – they'd never seen that before.

The girl with the story of the world under her skin.

They also came to know her as the girl with the flat feet, for she could walk kilometers on end, and did, all the way to Cape Reinga, wrapped in her own gleaming silence.

They knew one day she'd get up and walk, and be gone.

Because a god of far away would call to her, or maybe it was something else – no one could be sure. No one asked since she never spoke – and an answer to the Why was not possible. But the Why was not part of the story, not here, not now. Later, much later, there would perhaps be an answer to a million whys but for now everyone took it as something given: this girl was meant to stay as long as she did, and a voice called to her from across the seas, or from deep in the earth, or from even deeper in her very bones, and the wind carried guidelines for which way to roam.

Geography

BOOK NOTES, AGE 34
Wise Blood – Flannery O'Connor

> I keep coming to this: The idea that where you come from no longer exists, that where you might have gone – but didn't – was never really there. Place – what is it anyway? The idea of place in this world is not something you'll solve, for it is as elusive as life itself: place (like time) is not a physical thing but something you carry within.

The children ask where in the world they live, and it's a fair question. They've been moving most of their lives. They started in a faraway island, a place where their father still lives, in the South Pacific. It's where their whare is, where their whānau waits for them to return. That's one half of their family – the half that is connected to one place, one island, one coastline, one silty soil. The other half is in the far north of the American continent, in a place sweetly called Maine, but they've spent so little time there they barely know it.

She answers in various ways, none of them related to extended family in a real place on this real earth, none of them satisfactory to someone who might expect a concrete place name, an answer that situates oneself in terms of latitude and longitude, direction and geology, but all in ways the girls have come to expect.

Nobody owns me – for who am I?

That is a typical answer. From one of Mother's reliable philosopher-companions: Pippi Longstocking, a girl who dispenses small kernels of wisdom when the situation suits. The answer to this riddle, of course (both girls know it as certain as they know anything): the sea.

Sometimes the reply may be a muttering from Yeats – she frequently quotes lines about lingering wretchedly among insubstantial things. Or – a favourite riff off Norton Juster:

You know we exist at the beginning and the end of all things – the center and its very edges or

> *Your questions are always so complicated but really it's quite simple* (another favourite, borrowed from the wisdom of Dr Seuss)

or

> *Love the world, and you will survive, and thrive* (which is not really an answer to the question at all but rather an idea Mother frequently likes to throw at her children, to remind them to live and love equally, never mind where they *actually* are).

It is always a game – and a delight – to see what their mother might say, sometimes even pulling longer answers from her notebooks, though even those are only ever approximations of an answer to the central question about geography.

Other times she might not answer with words but stand firm and straight, her flat feet planted in the ground where they are – wherever they are, which could be Pakistan or Borneo, Turkey or Belize – and hold her hands to her chest. This is her sign for home.

The daughters have never heard her real voice, but they know the sound of her. She has been speaking to them their whole lives: hands and feet, head and shoulders. She has a language of her own, and it tells them things no matter where they are.

Even so, they like to ask.

Where in the world do we live, Ma?

Sometimes she points to something small: a dandelion, a puddle. When she points to it, they know they must lean in close and examine it. They know they can't feel it like she does, for they have come to understand that she feels the smallest of vibrations beyond what they sense: the moment the fibers of the dandelion separate and the wispy florets take flight on the summer breeze, the moment that same breeze lands on the puddle and lifts the surface and then almost imperceptible wavelets shimmy from one side to the other. But they lean in close and look, and wait for the movement that is about to occur. And when it does – when the dandelion wisps, when the wavelets whisper – they look up and see the intensity on their mother's face, and they understand: *we live here, in this dandelion's flight, in this puddle's purr.*

Birthday

BOOK NOTES, AGE 80
The Shadow of the Sun – Ryszard Kapuściński

> I'm an old woman by European standards. But here, I've lost track of counting. This continent is home – as much as anywhere – and my years have grown shapeless. Newton's time is absolute. Here, time is loose, an idea that stretches, elongates, even diffuses into thin air. Yes. Time is something that is real only if we think about it. Only if we have something that occupies our minds, for which time matters. For time to mean anything, it needs human energy and will, to push at it, to shape it.
>
> Time is a concept – our concept. As subjective as anything else: it depends on how you look at it, how you see it. And, I would add, how you listen to it.

It is time, they say. *You've been here too long, Nana. Time to come home. Mum, please.*

They are all here. They have gathered from oceans away, from the southern Pacific, from the northern Atlantic. They bring, mainly, the only gift suitable for her: themselves. Her two children, their children and their children, nieces and nephews and others who belong too. They swarm in with loud planes. She can hear them coming across sea miles and the great continent that is her home.

For five days they gather and celebrate. There are a great many feasts, and long nights of storytelling and music. For her part, she tunes into the smallest of stories and the most remote voices – the ones who don't share so easily, the ones not accustomed to making themselves heard. Little Lucy. And Pete. And her namesake: quiet Hanna.

She stays with them in their beach accommodation, but she misses her own simple dwelling. And so during the third night, she leaves the merry group around the bonfire and walks up the beach, finds a soft round indent, and lays her body down.

It's her granddaughter, the first one, who finds her there and sits down next to her. *Come home, Nana,* Iona says. *You've been away long enough.*

She hears the same thing many times during the rest of the visit. *Come with us. Come back. Come home.*

And: *It's time.*

She listens and considers it. Part of her may even desire it. But she hears the piercing blue sky even more, and the rumble under her feet, and she knows this place holds her future, which is immeasurably vast.

Soon they leave for their jobs, their schedules, their clocks that determine all the days of their lives. She has been here long enough to understand that time does not determine anything, that her direction is set by the hues of the hills to the south, the shade of the large mango in her garden, the songbirds who call each morning.

Time is nothing. As unlikely as that sounds, at her age.

After they leave, she opens the crate her daughters have left – as if they already knew her answer.

She recognises the old cedar chest – it sat for many years in her parents' bedroom in a place that almost no longer exists for her, a place so remote from her own life that she can see it only in the far reaches of her imagination. Maine. A place she loved once, but never belonged to. A place so far away, temporally and physically, that it almost isn't real. And yet. It *is* real – for that longago place is also right here, right now, for isn't it all right here, right now?

Inside the chest are special linens and items from her childhood: first shoes, brittle baby teeth, a locket of hair hanging on a gossamer gold thread. There are other things, too, and as her crooked fingers stroke the softness of her past, memories pour liquid across her mind. The memories are small and malleable, but moments that endure. How much time has passed? Time is nothing. Eighty candles on her birthday cake: small waxy things. Inconsequential, really. The items before her transcend. Like this blanket here, its blues and greens faded but the muscular fibers of earthtones still running through it.

That night, she sleeps outside again; she has missed the way the night buzzes and coos and sometimes, always in the distance, roars.

Crazy! They'd all said. *Sleeping outside! Here!? At your age!?*

Now, under the blanket that Aunt Zettie made for her back when she was – two, was it? – atop her woven matt on the thin grassy patch beyond her dirt yard, she is at peace. The blanket smells of a world that comes alive again – as familiar as the touch of her mother's palm, the smell of her father's hair gel, her sister's favourite sweater, her brother's catcher's mitt. All of it still real.

She is small under the blanket, so small: *Little Zettie*. She pulls her legs and feet up under it and all her muscle memory works in her favour: soon she is completely covered, toes and fingers curled in tight, elbows and knees safely hidden away. She closes her eyes. Time melts; she is Zettie, at seven.

She hears a giraffe softly sigh, drifts to sleep under the heat of the diamond light from all the stars in heaven.

When reading aloud to your children

BOOK NOTES, AGE 31
Polar Bear, Polar Bear, What Do You Hear? – Bill Martin Jr and Eric Carle

> I never tire of this book, even if I know the contents as well as if I'd written them myself. There's a polar bear and a lion, a hippo and a flamingo.
>
> Circularity and connectedness.
>
> Little Zettie, Little Zettie, what do you hear? I hear the bees buzzing in my ear.

When reading aloud to your children, speak in a clear voice so they understand every word.

When reading aloud to your children, soften your voice so the children, especially the very young ones, feel safe.

When reading aloud to your children, don't let your mind wander; let yourself sink into the story and enjoy it too; be present.

When reading aloud to your children, be sure to keep the book you are holding from monkeys who may swoop down from the trees to snatch it up.

When reading aloud to your children, choose a place outside that is upwind of the village rubbish heap, especially when it's burning, but downwind of the lemon tree and the clothesline.

When reading aloud to your children, do not sit under the coconut palm.

When reading aloud to your children, breathe through your nose.

Zettie writes these notes in her journal: it's how she would read to her children if she did read to her children. She adds another note now:

When reading aloud to your children, focus your mind away from the buzzing in your ear. You can never block it out entirely – but don't let it worry you. It has been there long before you existed, and it will carry on long after your own time here on earth.

It's the only time she's wanted to speak – to read with her children. She has no need for speaking, generally; days happen whether she speaks or not. She prefers to listen. But if she did read aloud to her children, she'd follow the above guidelines, and she'd also project her voice so it would carry out into the world, so it, too, could become a wave on the wind, endless and free.

Ways of seeing

BOOK NOTES, AGE 20
Ways of Seeing – John Berger

> Naked strips everything away: naked is the true self, whole and with no frills.
> No trim, no cover or cover-up.

When she met Rangi he told her he was of the sky. He said, *What's your story?* and she looked away, picked up her pencil, scribbled. He said, *I'll tell you mine.* He said, *You can see it here* and pointed to the story spiralling up an arm and meandering down a muscled leg. It looked to be a story of infinite possibilities, the swirls and curves hard to follow in one glance, needing closer inspection, and time, to arrive at their central truths. She pulled out a book she was reading – a history of the Pacific Isles – and he laughed, said, *No book is gonna make you get me.* She raised an eyebrow. He asked, now fierce:

What book should I read to understand you? She felt a burning sensation moving up her neck.

He took her to the beach and made her close her eyes and breathe. So loud were the sounds of fish dancing through water, crabs digging into sand, seagulls' swooping wings as they searched the shoreline for their evening meal. He took her to the bush and made her close her eyes and breathe. She listened to the tui and the swaying treefern and later that night lay awake on her floor while one morepork called across the lagoon to another. He took her to his mother's and sat her at the large kauri table, made her close her eyes and breathe. She waited for someone to say something, eager for their stories. They did not tell her much but passed plates of food that warmed her belly and made her smile.

Finally, he said, *See?* His turn to raise an eyebrow.

He came to her place late in the evening and found her reading. He sat on the floor across the room, leaned his strong back against the wall and said, *You won't get any closer to understanding me with that book.* She shrugged. He said, *How can you breathe with all those books? How can you see through all those words? Did you learn nothing from the beach, the bush?*

She shifted.

He said, *Did you learn nothing at my mother's table?*

Her palms sweated.

He said, *And when are you going to tell me your story?*

He was right: she was unwilling to wear her whakapapa on her skin or let him look any closer at her though she felt his eyes piercing like needles.

Then he rose and in one swift leap reached a place on the floor next to her. He laid a hand on her brow, her cheek. He moved his fingers down her neck. She flushed. He found the scar under her chin, rubbed his thumb gently back and forth, back and forth.

See? he said. *Let me and I will find you.* He kissed her. *I want to know your story,* he said.

He moved through her that night, and she let him: hands over body, body in hands.

She knew it would take years to understand him and even longer for him to understand her, but she found herself thinking for the first time that *here* was a man who knew how to look.

Dirt

BOOK NOTES, AGE 45
The Shadow of the Sun – Ryszard Kapuściński
    and
The Tree Where Man Was Born – Peter Matthiessen

> This continent is punctuated by light: bright, exquisite. The sun, in all directions, in all ways. Always. And then there is the landscape – whole terrains, alert with movement, with life.
>
> Inescapable light – inescapable earth.

The very smell of it makes her strong. There is life and death in this loamy stuff, a call beyond her own mortal life and all the lives of her family, beyond children and grandchildren and great-grandchildren yet to come. The soil sings. The hills hum.

This is the year she'll go about living in this new cosmos.

This is the year her children will leave her for good, the year they will shape lives of their own.

This is the year she will decide to stop moving, to stay in one place, and live completely on her own again.

This is the year she will abandon the small cot in the corner of the room for the smooth dirt floor and sleep every night, her ear to the ground.

This is the year she wakes to exquisite light each day.

This is the year she knows the rumble that has been calling her whole life is here. Is near.

Dreamscape V:
earth and dust

She is earth, she is dirt. Dust and nothing more – but dust is everything. There is a singing in the soil, a hymn in the hills.

Purity

> BOOK NOTES, AGE 28
> Die Entdeckung der Langsamkeit / The Discovery of Slowness – Sten Nadolny
>   and
> The Golden Notebook – Doris Lessing
>
>> Refusing to rush, oh yes.
>> It is a choice. One can simply slow to a pace that satisfies in all ways.
>>
>> And refusing to stay bound to one thing – to allow our emotions to hold us – when what we really want is something bigger, something more.

It's when it's finally over and he leaves that she slows down to listen again. Now she has more quiet in her life. The few years with him have been joyous – but even that human kind of joy travels on a frequency that blocks, or at least muffles, everything else.

Now she takes time to feel the earth's movements again. She has been working on a translation of Sten Nadolny's *Die Entdeckung der Langsamkeit* – The Discovery of Slowness – and she keeps this simple idea in mind: the idea of not being rushed. There was a magic in being with Rangi, the way his gaze lifted her from the ground. She loved him, yes. But love is loud.

This is how she will carry forward, with all her senses. She will refuse to be rushed. She will slow herself so that she might see light and all its wavy hues; she will extend her fingertips to the soil and feel the cool coming up from below the blistering upper layers; she will peel the mango slowly and note its pungent spice as it wafts through her nasal cavity; she will taste it on her tongue, its ripeness in her throat. She will hear the ocean rollers even from inland hills, the flight of a hummingbird, the sleep of her children. Not the breathing, but the *sleep*: she will open her ears at night that she might not miss it.

Have you ever heard the sleep of a child? It is the colour of a soft melon, the smell of freshly mown grass. It moves through the night on a wave all its own, not a ping of a high pitch or the murmur deep in the lowest of registers, but something off the sound charts entirely, close to purity and beauty, as close as you can ever get.

A silence like no other

BOOK NOTES, AGE 46
The Tree Where Man Was Born – Peter Matthiessen

> On the mystery and might of this creature, who, above all others, shouts
>
> s i l e n c e.

She cries when she sees her first elephant in the wild. It is not like any other thing she's encountered, not anywhere in the world. It's not the trumpeting that amazes her – she has heard that for years already, even from cities of distant continents; she knows to expect it. It's not the playful follies at the watering hole, so whimsical and utterly gravity-defying for such immense beasts. It's not even the sad eyes, those eyes that tell a thousand stories in one glance. Her dark skin ripples with energy when she first encounters them, walking out into the bush and stumbling on them so unexpectedly close; she is tuned into the way her spine trembles and emits a quaking energy of her own, down through her feet and deep into the soft mud where she stands, her camera unmoved, her heart frozen. But what makes her cry – what brings the tears that don't stop for days – is the silence that fills the space between them: the vast heartache of their history, their echo of memory upon memory. As if it's her very own.

Gifts

BOOK NOTES, AGE 40
Women Writing Africa, Vol. 1 – M.J. Daymond, Dorothy Driver (eds.)

> Women's voices. Women speaking, shouting, singing...
>
> This land is vast, and the voices many. I am watching my daughters grow, and listening to them all.
>
> We spread ourselves over landscapes.
> We move across seas, move in our hearts.
>
> The world will hear. A song so loud – how could it not?

The children are gifted, it turns out. The first one with language, talking to anyone she can as they move in their nomadic life, pronouncing syllables as if she were a native speaker. In Malaysia and Guatemala, Norway and Peru, she adopts the local twangs and ticks and habits, and if you heard her from afar and closed your eyes to her long angular frame you'd mistake her for one who was born there, or there, or there. The second with music, floating through days on rhythms of drums, guitar, ukulele, flute. She can play them all, and she makes music as they move, her pack bulging and jangling with happy noise. They are collectors, both of them – greedy and open-hearted. Words and sounds can be found at the centre of all things, and spreading out across the edges, too, thinning to whispers but floating nevertheless, infinite.

They travel for years, the girls and their mother. Mother can't settle.

The girls will go on to higher education of their own and it will serve them well, in time. But for now, at night, they are both poets. One jotting in her small book and the other softly singing baby baboons to sleep.

Mother, meanwhile, tunes in to fissures in the earth, cracks opening halfway round the world. An immensity beyond imagining. In the morning she will tell them it's time to go.

Lalalala go the baby baboons.

Dreamscape VI:
all of it

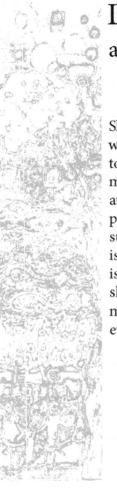

She is everything – air earth sky sea wind fire mountain river – flowing together and breaking apart, molecules forming and reforming at every possible second of every possible moment. All of it is surprising and new, and all of it is as ancient as the galaxies. She is asleep for this is a dream, but she is awake for this is life and she must always say yes – to life, to everything, to all of it.

Kinetic is a frame of mind, really

BOOK NOTES, AGE 55
The Shadow of the Sun – Ryszard Kapuściński

> Here, a whole universe.
> A place I can see and see and see. And feel under my feet.
> Dirt to stand on. An ocean to float in.
> A cosmos for me.

She's been kinetic, always. She's tired.

She first noticed how molecules move, how air vibrates, before she could speak. Long before she understood much about the quality of air, she could feel how waves stretch out across distances towards her, carrying low drumming or high humming or – her favourite – an earthen thrumming, a rumble so low no one else could hear it and so constant she began thinking of it as the *everrumble*. When she decided to stop talking (nearly fifty years back) it was because she knew – though she could not articulate it then – that this was related to the *everrumble*, that listening for it, to see where it would lead her, was the thing she needed to do.

So she did. Stop talking. Zettie, at seven.

She felt the energy of the world in motion from the earliest age, maybe from even before she emerged from her mother's womb. There was a screaming. And then, as a young girl, she learned to separate herself from the world: she learned that by placing a simple woollen blanket over her head, she could block out the rest; she could create a space where only her breath and heartbeat made up the rhythm of her existence. For some time, she lived under the blanket. Her parents found it most odd and her brother liked to throw his stuffed animals at her. Once he threw a book, just to see if it would make her move from her spot on the floor. But then he felt bad and came to sit beside her. He lifted the corner of the blanket to peer in – it had been nearly a year since she'd gone in there to live – and he was surprised at the tidy state, at her good-natured sense of things, even after having a book thrown at her.

It was at this very moment she was deciding whether to emerge and take another look at the world. A year is a long time to live under a blanket, after all. Still, it had done her good: while her parents had fretted over her mental and emotional well-being, she felt pretty fine. She wasn't going to explain it; she just understood intrinsically that the world was out of balance but that she, for her part, would not move one molecule of air to contribute to that imbalance. Living under a blanket gave her perspective, with its comforting earthy hues and holes between the knitted stitches that let in the diamond light. She liked that, the diamond light. She was not afraid under here. The world, in all its out-of-balance state, was out there, and she was here. There, here: what a difference a thin woollen blanket makes.

That was Zettie, at seven.

And then.

Her life unfolded, once she emerged from the blanket, as one might expect: there was a great deal of guesswork from the surrounding adults, attempts at diagnosis, arguments, hand-wringing. For her part, she just wanted to be a normal girl: listen to Stevie Nicks and Joni Mitchell and The Who and learn to Hula-hoop as well as her best friend Sally and enjoy that pressure that pushed down on her heart every time her brother's friend Scott was in her vicinity. Her heart cartwheeling: that was a new sensation. Eventually she grew up and led what appeared to anyone looking – to anyone not listening – a regular life, which included, if noted linearly in terms of chronology: childhood, puberty, college, university, love, children, divorce, career.

She vowed – perhaps between puberty and love – that she would stretch across time and space so as to thin herself flat so that bad things that happened had a lesser impact, and so she could see and feel the earth and its noise in a manner she could cope with. Staying in one place meant certain bombardment: sound from all angles, on all possible waves. So she pressed and pressed and eventually learned to stretch and expand herself around the globe. And her strategy worked, for the most part: she moved constantly, listening for the next suitable place. She found if she moved just enough she could dodge the wavelengths she did not like while allowing the soothing tones to sink in deep.

She moved as long as she had no reason to stop. Simple laws of physics: a body in motion, etc. Even here on this great continent – she has been here ten years – she's never stayed long in one place, residing in silty river deltas, in cooler mossy mountain forests. People might call it exotic, all this roaming. But really, no matter where she dwelled, which one place, it was as if she occupied many places at once, so multiple and layered were the noises that seeped in and enveloped her life.

Until she stopped. Why stop after so many years in motion? Simple laws of physics: something got in the way.

Here, across this vast land, the thrumming in the earth is constant. And now she's waiting. For what, she's not sure. For the thrumming to come closer, to get louder. She heard it first as a child, then intermittently through her nomadic life.

Now that she's here, she will hold still, open her ears more.

She flattens her molecules, lets them spill across the earth, reshape to follow the contours of this little anthill, that larger termite mound. She lies down and stretches her body, her limbs, her massive dark hair, connecting maximum surface area.

And she waits.

She has time.

Dreamscape VII: [untitled]

She listens and listens and listens. She hears all the sounds of the world, and she tastes all the sounds of the world, and she touches all the sounds of the world, and she feels all the sounds of the world. And she is all the sounds of the world.

Clarity

BOOK NOTES, AGE 105
Final Notations – Adrienne Rich

> How can I not be reading once more from the lines of Adrienne Rich, on this day of all days?

In her last day on earth, the old woman finally understands. The moment of clarity comes in the morning, and it is later in the day, just before the rapid darkening that is the tropical night, that she will die.

They say there might be a flash that quick-fires across your mind when you die, a connecting of images from your life. They say this could happen at the very end. This is not the case. She sits on her stone stoop in the early hours of dawn and opens her mind to the day, her last day. She breathes and sings to herself. She thinks of her daughters, her sister, her brother. She smiles at the arcing sun, the perfect geometry of the planets and stars. In the end, it's not her life she sees. No flashes of moments tucked away in memory. She's lived her life, after all. It need not be reviewed once more.

It's not so much a vision as a full-on worldly orchestral movement. Overtones and undercurrents. Chantings and crashings. Rowdy and dreadful but also melodious and beautiful. It happens in a flash, yes, but its layers are as deep as oceans, as wide as the space between stars. Complicated cadences, wave upon wave, some dissonant, some harmonious. Overlapping and straining and singing and screaming.

Screaming.

Dolphins birthing dying. Balugas breeching screeching. Bears clawing pawing. Giraffes chewing screwing. Birds calling spiralling. A tiger snuffling, an eagle ruffling. A lion lovemaking, a gibbon woop-wooping.

No dead noise – all alive. These are moments of animal expression, sometimes simultaneous, sometimes scant milliseconds apart. They invade her ears and smash her brain. Individual noises can be picked out: that traffic jam of penguins, horns honking on Antarctic ice; the pollywannacracker of a pet parrot in upstate New York; the quiet snort of a baby rhino newly born, soft and scared, not yet knowing his own power, and vulnerability.

And also: Shamu's scream.

That's it, finally: the screaming that accompanied her own wail as she slipped into the world, purple and slick from her mother's womb. She hears it now, again – a memory. She's sure. It's bright and terrible: Shamu calling to her own mother. Not something she hears, for the moment is past, but something reverberating still. A quick technological search would tell her that her birth day was the same day in October, 1965, that Shamu was captured while her mother drowned in front of her panicked eyes, stuck with a harpoon and bleeding violently from the great gash. But she does not need technology to understand the source of this noise, at last. An opening and a closing: her own emergence into the world, and an orca's cruel capture. A balance in the cosmic scale? No. But a message. A note on life and death. A buzzing. A murmur. A call.

An echo that will accompany her to her grave.

Born in northern Maine over a hundred years ago, just after the midpoint of the previous century, she lived the first part of her life roaming, dreaming, listening.

It's a strange thing, to listen.

Most people focus on what they see in front of them. Seers will see into the future.

But her gift has been to hear the minutest of leaf crackle and spider spinning, to hear a violin in Berlin hover over a lion's yawn reaching across the Serengeti plains.

The sounds that shake the earth.

And this. Shamu. She has heard Shamu all her life. And now she knows what to call it. This agony, this wailing.

Such cacophony.

The everrumble

BOOK NOTES, AGE 105
Charlotte's Web – E.B. White

> And then I recalled the most wonderfully succinct version of the way we occupy this space on earth, the way we come and go, the way we move through our time.
>
> A life: a birth... a death.
> And living. Yes.
> Living: Can you hear it?

And now they are coming. For her.

Her mind turns liquid, moves to a distant baobab, ancient and looming against the brilliant sky. Rustling. No, not rustling. Sighing? She pours her mind towards it. Breathing? She stretches, her fingertips making light contact with the gnarled bark, reaching into a crack. The crack opens wide enough for her head to poke through. The bark is the very smell of life. But oh: also, life fading. A hush settling on all senses.

The sound of death: everything and nothing, all echoes imaginable but then a silence that is deafening, a wide gaping naught.

The tree opens itself more; the cavern gawks. She climbs in, pulling her body inside, limb by limb.

It's quiet in here.

The tastesmellsoundfeelsight of death also emits, from inside the baobab, a dogged continuation of life – a livingdyingliving, over and over. An old Dinka song passes through the tree:

> *In the time when Dendid created all things,*
> *He created the sun,*
> *And the sun is born, and dies, and comes again.*
> *He created the moon,*
> *And the moon is born, and dies, and comes again;*
> *He created the stars,*
> *And the stars are born, and die, and come again;*
> *He created man,*
> *And man is born, and dies, and does not come again.*

She breathes in the circularity, the melting of linear perception, the quiet persistence of the whole. The fleeting moment of one small thing such as her life, which will end with certainty – this against the mighty foreverness of the baobab, standing sentinel on this plain more than a thousand years.

Tree of life.

Listen.

She climbs out and looks across the plain. Out in the distance: all the world's animals. She can hear their songs bursting through the baobab: the cry of the whale, the screech of the owl; a symphony of frogs, a stampede of wildebeest. A penguin pattering across ice, a hare darting over powder. The roar of the kingly lion, the suck of the lowly mosquito. The wingbeat of the weaver, and bees foreverbuzzing. They are alive – alive! Here in this tree.

Shaking the earth.

She has thought her purpose was to listen to death, to view it as the inevitable way the story ends. Death, pulsing a familiar pattern, a long continuous noise. But now, in the moment of her own fading, she senses from the shade of the baobab: these animals who have been reaching across space and time are going to *live*.

So this is why she is here. This place, where humans were born, and where they have demolished themselves savagely. For life, for hope. The mighty earth will live; the incessant and rowdy clamour of life itself will grow and grow and grow. Whether her own kind will grow with it she cannot know. But she hears now – louder than bombs, than rockets, than missiles, than all the dead noises that have filled her world for 105 years – the enduring patterns, more vast and expansive than anything humankind has built up or broken down.

Ancient shapes looming in the west, great shadows – awesome, enchanted – under the pink light of late afternoon. A memory of elephants.

She feels the *everrumble*. The heartbeat of every living creature, so loud it's hurting her ears. They'll soon start bleeding. And why not? Her form will turn to liquid, then dust. Blood is just blood. It's nothing. It's nothing.

Her body pulsates. The skin of her long arms flaps and frays in the breeze. Is it peeling way? Will it fly off, leaving her meat and bones for the jackals? Is this what death feels like? No. Wait. Her skin is not shedding: it moves in long, rhythmic motions. Seismic rumbles emanate up through her feet.

Her skin is dancing. Telling the story of the world.

Is it time? Should she let go? She is so old, so old. She will die here, today. A mere life, a mere death. That is all. She will not complain. She is ready.

An elephant lifts her great foot and brings it down. Molecules of dust explode upward and drift, slowly, glimmering, covering the earth with a thin blanket of warmth. The earthy smell is golden and red. Ancient dust and light. The old woman is showered by a spray of colour: blues of sky, the reassuring oranges and yellows of sweet papaya and mango. The dust hovers and blankets the wide plain: a covering of primeval soil. It settles and is scratchy on her skin but the whole effect of lying under it is a smooth muffling.

She is lost in reverie, or memory. *How comforting is the world under cover – those earthy hues touched by the sparkling diamond light.*

All the elephants in the world are alert, feet flat to the ground, trunks softly curled and brushing the warm earth. The old woman stands, pushes down through her feet and feels energy flow up through the bones of her legs. Her chest feels as if it will burst.

Infrasound connecting her at last.

The *everrumble*, glorious.

She catches the distinct smell of piss: the elephants are joyous. She looks down at her own moving skin, at her feet which have flattened over the years. Her mind is solid, liquid, air; memory is life.

Oh thundering sound, my heart! Hold steady, my breath!

She lifts one of her sure flat feet, takes a step towards them.

Acknowledgements

Thank you to:

Christopher Allen, Nod Ghosh, Tania Hershman, Gail Ingram, Frankie McMillan, Catherine McNamara, James Norcliffe, Sam Rasnake, Robert Scotellaro and Tracey Slaughter, for draft reading and encouragement;

Iona Winter and Georgina Harris Hill, for language fine-tuning;

Jude Higgins and the team at Ad Hoc Fiction, for sharing Zettie's world – and to John, for the beautiful book design;

Eyayu Genet, for his painting;

and my daughters, Lola and Jana – I am stronger in life and on the page because of you.

Grateful acknowledgement to the editors of the following journals where earlier versions of these chapters previously appeared:

Bath Flash Fiction Award and *To Carry Her Home: Bath Flash Fiction Vol 1* – Dreamscape I: whale shark and boy

Flash: The International Short-short Story Magazine – The slap

Further acknowledgement to the following for materials referenced:

Houghton Mifflin Harcourt, for Ursula LeGuin, *A Wizard of Earthsea*

Penguin Random House, for Peter Matthiessen, *The Tree Where Man Was Born*

Puffin/Penguin Random House, for Michael Ende, *Momo*

About the Author

MICHELLE ELVY is a writer, editor and manuscript assessor based in New Zealand, living and travelling aboard her sailboat *Momo* for more than fifteen years. She is Assistant Editor for the *Best Small Fictions* series (published in the US). She also edits at *Flash Frontier: An Adventure in Short Fiction* and chairs New Zealand's National Flash Fiction Day. In 2018, she edited, with Frankie McMillan and James Norcliffe, *Bonsai: Best small stories from Aotearoa New Zealand* (Canterbury University Press). Her poetry, fiction, travel writing, creative nonfiction and reviews have been widely published and anthologised. This is her first book of collected works. More at michelleelvy.com

About the Artist

Eyayu Genet was born in Durbete, Ethiopia, 470 km north of the capital city, Addis Ababa. He earned his Bachelor's Degree in Economics from Bahir Dar University in 2007. That same year, he joined the Addis Ababa University Alle School of Fine Arts and Design and received his BFA degree in painting with great distinction in 2011. In recent years, he has put energy into making the city of Bahir Dar an alternative art corner in the nation, organizing numerous art shows and training 80 students in technical and artistic expression. Currently, he is an art instructor at the Bahir Dar University. More at thenextcanvas.com/eyayu-genet

Story Index

A silence like no other 86
Because 46
Before the bees 25
Birthday. 70
Book Notes 27
Cartwheels 13
Cartwheels, again 34
Clarity 97
Comfort of a cool pine floor. 5
Dirt. 81
Dreamscape I: whale shark and boy 10
Dreamscape II: moon and sea 24
Dreamscape III: willow and moon. 31
Dreamscape IV: bird and warrior 62
Dreamscape V: earth and dust 83
Dreamscape VI: all of it. 90
Dreamscape VII: [untitled] 96
Fidelity 20

Geography 66
Gifts 88
Higher education 57
Kinetic is a frame of mind, really 91
Light and shadow 3
Peek-a-boo 8
Pressure drop, or:
Sea World, August 1971, Part 2 38
Purity 84
Sea World: August 1971 23
Silence 32
Soothsayer 51
Specialists 42
The bees 15
The everrumble 101
The first screaming 18
The slap 40
Under the Aotearoa sun 63
Ways of seeing 78
When reading aloud to your children 75